OCTOPUSES

Heinemann Library
Chicago, Illinois

Darlene R. Stille

Designed by Kimberly Saar, Heinemann Library
Illustrations and maps by John Fleck
Photo research by Bill Broyles
Originated by Ambassador Litho Ltd.
Printed by Wing King Tong in Hong Kong

07 06 05 04 03
10 9 8 7 6 5 4 3 2 1

Library of Congress Cataloging-in-Publication Data
Stille, Darlene R.
  Octopuses / Darlene R. Stille.
     p. cm. -- (Sea creatures)
Summary: Describes the physical characteristics and behavior of octopuses, as well as ways in which scientists study them.
Includes bibliographical references (p.   ).
  ISBN 1-40340-959-5 (HC), 1-4034-3563-4 (pbk.)
 1. Octopus--Juvenile literature. [1. Octopus.] I. Title. II. Series.
  QL430.3.O2 S884 2003
  594'.56--dc21

                    2002010622

Acknowledgments
The author and publishers are grateful to the following for permission to reproduce copyright material:

Cover photograph by David B. Fleetham/Seapics.com

Title page, icons Art Womack/Pictor International; pp. 4, 27 Jeffrey Rotman/Seapics.com; pp. 5, 23 Bob Cranston/Seapics.com; pp. 6, 15B, 29 Doug Perrine/Seapics.com; pp. 8, 20 David B. Fleetham/Seapics.com; p. 9 Gregory Ochocki/Seapics.com; pp. 10, 12 Norbert Wu Photography; p. 11 David J. Wrobel/Monterey Bay Aquarium Foundation; pp. 13, 18 Fred Bavendam/Minden Pictures; p. 14 Mike Severns/Seapics.com; pp. 15T, 19 Clay Bryce/Seapics.com; p. 16 Brandon D. Cole; p. 17 Masa Ushioda/Seapics.com; p. 21 A. & C. Mahaney/Seapics.com; p. 22 Dr. James B. Wood; p. 24 Flip Nicklin/Minden Pictures; p. 25 Glen M. Oliver/Visuals Unlimited; p. 26 Robert F. Sisson/National Geographic Society; p. 26 Visuals Unlimited; p. 28 Brandon D. Cole

Special thanks to Dr. James Woods of the National Resource Center of Cephalopods in Galveston, Texas, for his help in the preparation of this book.

Every effort has been made to contact copyright holders of any material reproduced in this book. Any omissions will be rectified in subsequent printings if notice is given to the publisher.

Some words are shown in bold, **like this.** You can find out what they mean by looking in the glossary.

Contents

How Would You Find a Giant Octopus? 4

Is It a Head or a Body? 6

How Many Kinds of Octopuses Are There? 10

Where Do Octopuses Live? .12

What Does an Octopus Eat? 14

How Does an Octopus Protect Itself? 16

Does an Octopus Have a Family? 21

Are Octopuses Endangered? 25

How Do We Learn About Octopuses? 26

Fact File 28

Glossary 30

More Books to Read 31

Index 32

How Would You Find a Giant Octopus?

You join a team of scientists, called marine biologists, who study octopuses in the Pacific Ocean. They know that some of the huge animals live off the coast of Oregon.

You need the right equipment

You ride a boat to a place that the marine biologists know is home to some octopuses. You put on a tight-fitting wet suit made of a rubbery material that will keep your body warm in the cold water. After a final check of your **SCUBA** gear, you put the air tank on your back like a backpack. SCUBA stands for Self-Contained Underwater Breathing Apparatus. The metal tank is filled with a mixture of gases that take the place of the air you normally breathe. A hose connects the tank to a mouthpiece so that you can breathe underwater.

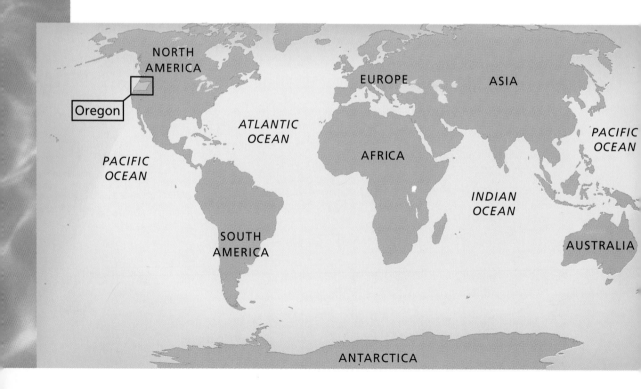

A scientist diving in the deep, cold waters of the northern Pacific ocean comes face to face with a giant Pacific octopus. If the diver leaves the octopus alone, there is nothing to fear.

A glass diving mask covers your eyes so you can see underwater. Rubber fins on your feet help you swim. Your team members carry bright lights to help you see in the dark water. You are diving at night when octopuses come out to feed.

You need to be in the right place

You jump into the water and slowly sink toward the ocean floor. Near the bottom, everyone stops. Right below you is an amazing sight. It looks like a leather bag with eight long arms. It's a giant Pacific octopus.

Suddenly, the giant octopus turns its big eyes toward you. Will those long arms reach out like a monster in a story and grab you? Don't worry. The giant Pacific octopus, like all octopuses, is very shy. It squirts a cloud of dark **ink** at you and disappears in the darkness.

Is It a Head Or a Body?

The octopus's "body" looks like it should be the head. The head is where you might think the body begins. A giant Pacific octopus looks like a big, soft, round bean bag crawling around on the ocean floor.

It's a head-foot

The octopus is a kind of animal called a **cephalopod.** The word *cephalopod* comes from Greek words that mean "head" and "foot." Squid and cuttlefish are also cephalopods.

Cephalopods belong to a group of animals called **mollusks.** Mollusks are **invertebrates,** or animals that do not have backbones. In fact, mollusks do not have any bones at all. Some mollusks have shells to protect their soft bodies. Clams and snails are mollusks that have hard, outer shells. The octopus does not have a shell.

The chambered nautilus is a relative of the octopus.

6

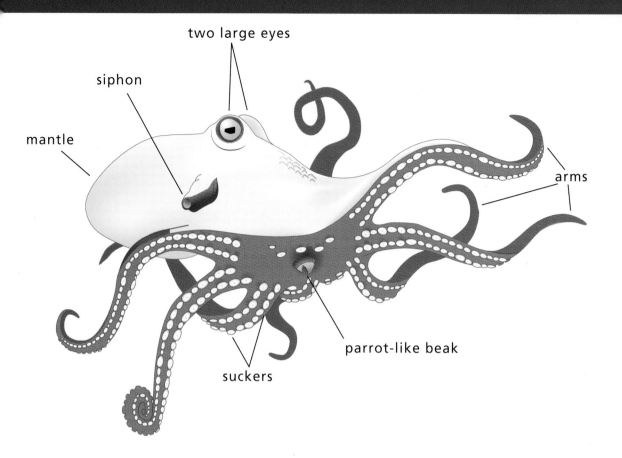

two large eyes

siphon

mantle

arms

parrot-like beak

suckers

It's a bag without bones

The bag-like structure is called the **mantle**. This is the octopus's "body." It is made of muscle and is the only thing that protects the soft internal organs. Two eyes sit just below the mantle. The area between the eyes is the head. This is where the brain is.

The mantle contains the octopus's heart, digestive system, and other internal organs. Between the inside of the bag and the internal organs, there is a space called the mantle cavity. The octopus has **gills** inside the **mantle cavity.** Fish and almost all other animals that spend their lives in the water use gills to breathe. The octopus sucks water into the cavity through slits in the mantle. The gills take oxygen from this water and send it to the octopus's blood.

The octopus has lots of heart

An octopus has three hearts. A heart at the end of each **gill** takes in blood from tiny blood vessels. As the blood is pumped through the gills, it picks up oxygen from the water. The third heart then gets this blood and pumps it through the octopus's body.

After the gills take oxygen from the water, muscles in the mantle force the water back out through a tube called a **siphon.** Then the gills take in a fresh supply of water with oxygen.

It has amazing arms

An octopus's arms bend and twist in all directions. Two rows of powerful **suckers** cover the underside of each arm and can hold onto rocks. Octopuses that live on the ocean floor use their arms to crawl on the ocean floor and into cracks and under rocks.

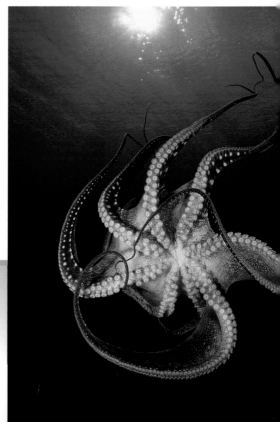

Each sucker has special nerve cells called **chemoreceptors.** The chemoreceptors sense substances in the water, just as our noses sense substances in the air. The suckers also let the octopus feel and taste the world around it.

*The eight arms of an octopus join together under the **mantle** around the octopus's mouth.*

Each arm is covered with suckers that look like suction cups. The powerful suckers can grab rocks or hold on to prey. The suckers can also feel, taste, and smell.

An octopus's web

An octopus's arms are made mostly of muscle. They are connected under the mantle by a piece of skin called the **webbing.** In the center of the webbing is the octopus's mouth. The mouth is a hard, sharp **beak** that looks like the beak of a parrot.

True Blue

An octopus's blood is blue, not red. Human blood is red because it has hemoglobin, which turns red when it attaches to the oxygen it carries to the body's cells. Octopus blood has a substance called hemocyanin, which does not bind, or connect, as easily to oxygen.

How Many Kinds of Octopuses are There?

It can be hard to find octopuses, but scientists think there are about 150 different kinds. New **species** are still being discovered. The waters off of Australia may have more kinds of octopuses than anywhere else in the world.

The common octopus

There really is an octopus species called the common octopus. It lives all over the world in warm waters. Other octopuses that are closely related to the common octopus include the 30-foot (9-meter) giant Pacific octopus and the tiny Californian octopus that is only about one inch (two and a half centimeters) long. All of these octopuses belong to a group called the Incirrata.

This Californian octopus, from arm tip to arm tip, is smaller than your little finger.

A giant Pacific octopus can be a scary sight. Its arms are long enough to wrap around a car. The giant Pacific octopus is the largest octopus known.

Unusual octopuses

Octopuses in the **cirrata** group live in the open ocean as far down as three miles (five kilometers). They have **webbing** that starts at the mantle and goes almost to the tips of their arms. The extra webbing gives cirrate octopuses a bell shape. They also have two small fins on their mantle. Scientists do not know very much about cirrate octopuses. They are hard to find and study.

This cirrate octopus looks like a big hat. Cirrate octopuses have cirri, which are rows of thin, hair-like organs, on their arms instead of suckers. They also have fins that help them swim.

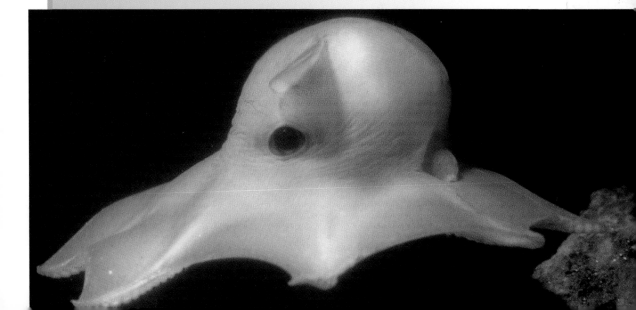

Where Do Octopuses Live?

Octopuses live in the salty water of seas and oceans all over the world. Some are **benthic.** That means they live on the ocean bottom. Others are **pelagic** and float in the open ocean at different depths.

Benthic habitats

The ocean has different depths at different places. The bottom of the ocean is shallower near the coast. A coastal benthic octopus might live at a depth of 650 feet (200 meters). That's about two times as far as a football field. But far out in the ocean, the bottom may be as deep as 3,300 feet (1,000 meters).

Benthic waters can be warm or cold. The giant Pacific octopus is a cold-water benthic **species** that lives in deep water. Some common octopuses live in shallow water off the coast of Florida. The water here is warmer.

This is an Antarctic octopus. This very small species lives only in the Southern Hemisphere. It eats tiny shrimp and other crustaceans.

A tin can or a broken bottle can make a snug, safe home for an octopus. Some octopuses build dens in sand or under rocks. An octopus may also move into an empty den that was built by another octopus.

Pelagic habitats

Any water that is not near the shore is pelagic, or open ocean water. These waters are usually cold. Pelagic octopus species can also be found at different depths. Many of the **cirrata** octopuses are pelagic.

Visiting an octopus home

Most octopuses build their homes on the mud, sand, or gravel of the ocean floor. An octopus home is called a **den.** The den might be a hole under a rock or in a pile of rocks. Octopuses like a den with an opening that is hard to get into. Small octopuses have even been known to make use of a rusty tin can or an old bucket for a den. Any place that an octopus can crawl into and hide makes a good home.

? **Did you know?**

An octopus can squeeze through a hole as small as its beak.

What Does an Octopus Eat?

The octopus is a **predator.** It eats other animals. The octopus hunts mainly at night.

Octopuses love seafood

The favorite foods of an octopus are fish, clams, crabs, shrimp, and snails. Except for fish, these sea animals have hard shells, but that is not a problem for an octopus. Sometimes the octopus uses its arms and suckers to pull the shell apart.

An octopus can also use its sharp **beak** to break the shell or to punch a hole in the shell. Or, it can drill a hole in the shell with its strange tongue, or **radula.** The radula is covered with tiny, rough teeth. Then the octopus puts its saliva, which contains a poison, into the shell. The poison makes it difficult for the **prey** to keep moving, so it is easier for the octopus to eat it.

Octopus trash

After an octopus has eaten, it puts the shells just outside the opening of its **den.** The shells pile up in a heap called a **midden.** Divers looking for octopus dens look for middens.

*An octopus grabs a **mollusk** with its suckers and tucks the animal under its mantle.*

14

Middens help scientists learn what an octopus has been eating.

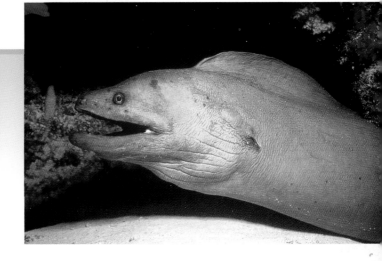

The long, snake-like body of the moray eel can squeeze inside the den of an octopus.

Some animals like to eat octopuses!

Many animals like to eat octopus. Octopuses provide food for seals, whales, sharks and other large fish, and moray eels. Only larger predators can catch a large octopus.

Octopuses also provide food for people. Divers use spear guns to hunt octopus. Octopuses are sometimes caught with fishing lures and in nets or traps. Cooks use the **mantle** and arms of an octopus in recipes. Sometimes they fry the octopus. Sometimes they use octopus in sauces. People have been eating octopus for thousands of years.

How Does an Octopus Protect Itself?

One way for an octopus to keep safe is to use **camouflage** and "disappear." Another way is to be alert and avoid danger. Octopuses also have other methods of defense.

Mimicry is another type of camouflage. The mimic octopus was discovered in 1998. This one has shaped its body like a mantis shrimp.

It is a master of disguise

Octopuses can use **cryptic camouflage** to hide from **predators.** They change their skin color and texture to match their **habitat.** Some octopuses can do this in only a second. Special cells in their skin, called **chromatophores,** make it possible for octopuses to change color. An octopus can have hundreds of chromatophores in an area of skin no bigger around than the tip of a pencil eraser.

Special muscles let an octopus fold its skin to look rough, like rocks, or smooth, like sand. An angry octopus can make the skin on top of its **mantle** stick up to look like horns.

The Caribbean reef octopus can make itself blend in with the colors of a coral reef.

An octopus squirts a cloud of dark ink into the water.
The diver has bothered the octopus by holding on to it.

It confuses the enemy

Another octopus trick is to send out a cloud of dark **ink.**
Inside an octopus's mantle is an organ called an ink sac.
The sac contains ink that is usually colored black or dark
brown. If a predator, such as a shark, is after an octopus,
the octopus can squirt ink out of the ink sac.

The ink mixes with the water to create a dark cloud around
the octopus. Sometimes the ink cloud takes on the shape
of the octopus's body. The shark cannot see the octopus
because of the dark ink cloud. The shark becomes confused.
This gives the octopus time to get away.

An octopus *is* always alert

An octopus cannot hear (no ears!), but its body can feel vibrations. It can feel the vibrations of a boat, a swimmer, or a **predator** coming toward it. If an octopus feels threatened, it first tries to hide in its **den** or in the crack of a rock.

The octopus can raise its eyes up above its mantle like two stalks. This lets the octopus peek outside of its den without exposing its body. Sometimes it just raises up one eye. Octopuses can see objects as well as you can, but they cannot see colors. However, octopuses can see very well at night.

A giant Pacific octopus props itself up to take a look around.

The deadly blue-ringed octopus has colorful blue rings all over its body. The blue-ringed octopus has venom, or poison, that can kill a human being.

Protection by Attracting Attention

Like all octopuses, the blue-ringed octopus from Australia is shy and will hide when people or predators appear. But if it feels threatened, bright blue-colored rings flash across its skin. These rings mean "Stay away or else!"

Swimmers and divers should never try to pick up a blue-ringed octopus or pull the octopus from its den. The blue-ringed octopus can bite and inject a powerful venom, or poison. A small amount of this venom is strong enough to kill ten average-size adults!

Jetting away

When it is in great danger, the octopus does not use its arms to crawl away. The octopus makes its body behave like the engine of a jet airplane. A jet takes in air and shoots it out the back of the engine. The octopus does the same thing with water.

First, the octopus takes in water through the two slits in its head. The water fills the **mantle cavity.** Then, the octopus uses the muscles of its **mantle** to push the water out of its **siphon.** A jet of water shoots backward out of the octopus. The force of the jet sends the octopus forward. With its long arms trailing behind, the octopus jets away to the safety of a hole in a rock or its **den.**

*If an octopus cannot avoid a **predator** by hiding, using camouflage, or shooting **ink,** it will try to escape by jetting away. This is a day octopus.*

Does an Octopus Have a Family?

There is no such thing as an octopus family of mother, father, and little octopuses. Every octopus lives by itself in its own den.

A male mates with a female octopus. The octopus reproduces through sexual reproduction.

The octopus is a loner

Octopuses don't get together very much. They live alone, hunt alone, and eat alone.

Scientists once thought that octopuses never gathered together in groups. Then some scientists reported that they had seen young red octopuses in a group called a **school.** Fish often gather in schools for protection. That may be why the red octopuses did it. No one knows for sure. The red octopus is the only type of octopus that scientists have seen in schools, but there may be other types of octopus that school.

Octopuses do get together to mate

Octopuses reproduce sexually. Sperm from a male octopus must fertilize the eggs of a female octopus.

The male octopus has a special arm used for mating. This arm is shorter than his other seven arms. The male octopus uses his short arm to place a packet of sperm inside the mantle of a female octopus.

Each egg has lots of company

The female uses the sperm to fertilize her eggs. She strings the eggs together. Then she hangs the strings of eggs in her **den.** The tiny dwarf octopus hangs hundreds of eggs and may use an empty clam shell for a den. A big octopus may hang thousands of eggs inside her den of rocks.

An octopus egg does not have a hard shell like the egg of a chicken. The shell is soft and transparent. This means you can see the little octopus inside a see-through egg.

A mother devoted to caring for eggs

A little octopus begins to grow inside each egg. The mother spends all of her time taking care of the eggs. She guards them from **predators,** such as starfish, that try to get into the den and eat the eggs. Even though the eggs are already underwater, she sprays the eggs with more water to keep them clean and give them more oxygen.

The egg is soft and clear. You can see the baby octopus inside.

The giant Pacific octopus hangs her eggs inside her den. The mother spends all her time caring for the eggs. After the eggs hatch, the mother dies.

The mother octopus does not eat while she takes care of the eggs. She does not even sleep. When the baby octopuses hatch out of their eggs, the mother dies. Each baby octopus is then on its own.

The babies have to take care of themselves

A newborn octopus looks like an adult octopus, only much smaller. It can do everything an adult can do. It can change color. It can even squirt **ink.**

It is very important for a baby octopus not to be noticed by anything that might eat it. The newborn octopuses go to the surface of the ocean. They float around with lots of tiny plants and other small animals, which are called **plankton.**

Many baby octopuses get eaten by bigger animals. The ones that survive settle to the bottom and then grow up. They find an empty den or build a new one. They live alone until they mate, and then they die.

An octopus's life is short

Octopuses do not live very long. Small warm-water octopuses live about a year. Big octopuses, such as the giant Pacific octopus, usually live three years.

The eight arms can be clearly seen on a newly hatched baby octopus.

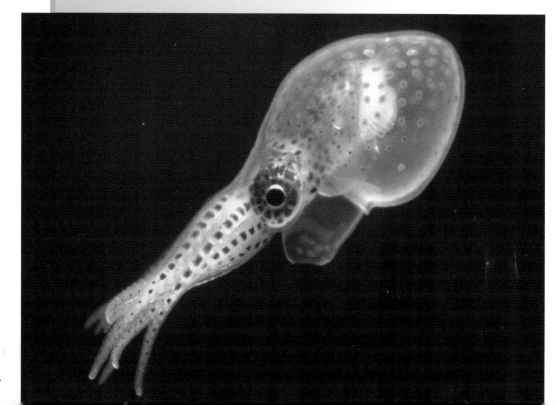

Are Octopuses Endangered?

No octopus species is on the list of endangered animals. But no one really knows for sure if they are safe.

No one knows for sure

It is very difficult to study octopuses. They are shy and hard to find and so are not easy to count. Scientists do not even know for sure how many kinds, or **species,** there are. They think there are about 150 octopus species worldwide.

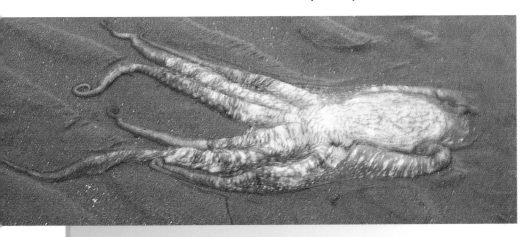

A dead octopus lies on a beach. No one knows for sure whether any species of octopus is endangered.

Could octopuses ever become endangered?

A species of octopus could become endangered if the octopuses die faster than they can reproduce. Ocean pollution that harms its **habitat** or kills the octopus's **prey** is also a concern.

Many people like to eat octopuses, but it is important not to catch too many. People who work in the pet trade like to catch the more attractive octopus species. This can also reduce the numbers of octopuses.

How Do We Learn About Octopuses?

Marine biologists observe octopuses that live in public **aquariums,** study them in laboratories, and try to find them in the oceans.

Studying octopuses in the oceans

Most scientists study octopuses in the ocean. They put on **SCUBA** gear and dive down to study how octopuses live in shallow water. They use little submarines to study octopuses that live in deep water. Sometimes scientists use robot submarines called **ROV's.** ROV stands for Remotely Operated Vehicle. ROV's have found new things about octopuses.

Not all octopuses live on the seafloor. Some octopuses float in the middle of the ocean. These octopuses do not live in dens. So they cannot lay eggs in dens. The female lays eggs under her long arms!

Scientists use ROV's to look for octopuses that live too far down for divers to go.

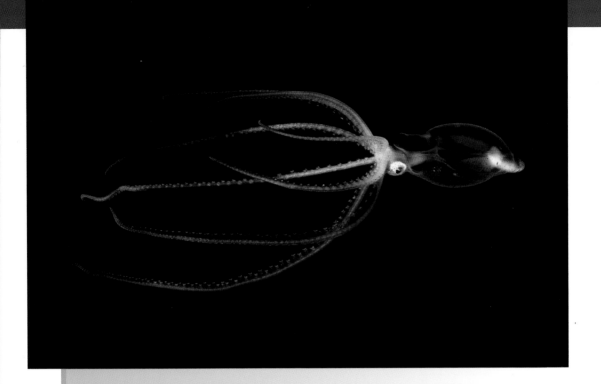

*The common blanket octopus lives in the Mediterranean Ocean and along both coasts of the North and South Atlantic Ocean. Scientists do not know much about this **species.***

Scientists need to learn more about octopuses. They want to know how many there are. Do all octopuses always live alone? How strong is the biggest octopus? How smart is the average octopus? There is much more to discover about these wonderful creatures of the sea.

Studying octopuses in the lab

Scientists agree that the octopus is the most advanced **invertebrate.** They are smart, but not in the same way that humans are smart. There have been some experiments to see if octopuses can learn by watching other octopuses do things, such as opening jars. Some scientists think the results show that octopuses can learn by watching. Others feel that more experiments are needed.

☑ The largest octopus is the giant octopus that lives in the Pacific Ocean. It can weigh up to 150 pounds (68 kilograms)—as much as an adult human being weighs. The distance from the tip of one arm to the tip of another can be 25 feet (seven and a half meters). Its arms are big enough to hug a car.

☑ The longer its arms, the more suckers an octopus has. The adult female giant Pacific octopus has a total of 2,240 suckers, 280 on each arm. An adult male has fewer suckers, because one of its arms is used for mating and is shorter than its other arms.

☑ If an octopus loses an arm, it can grow a new one, complete with suckers.

☑ An octopus's esophagus, or throat, goes through its brain.

☑ An octopus can be killed by its own **ink.** If an octopus in an aquarium squirts ink, the ink will cover its gills and it cannot breathe. The water must be changed right away.

This octopus is using its arms to walk on the sea bottom.

- Long ago, octopus ink was used as ink for pens.

- Not all octopuses can squirt ink. Most deep-sea octopuses do not have ink sacs.

- The color of an octopus can depend upon its mood. If an octopus turns white, it may be frightened. If it turns red, it may be angry.

This is a common day octopus. The yellow "tube" is the siphon.

- An octopus has two times as many nerves in its body as it has in its brain. This is because each sucker has nerves.

- The common octopus lays about 250,000 eggs—that is a quarter of a million eggs!

- An octopus has arms, not tentacles. Tentacles are used to catch prey. Some tentacles have claws or hooks. The squid is a cephalopod that has eight arms and two tentacles.

This is the same octopus. It has changed its color from white to brown in only a few seconds.

Glossary

aquarium tank where fish and other sea animals are kept

beak hard, sharp mouth of an octopus

benthic the bottom

camouflage way an animal hides

cephalopod type of animal that includes octopus, squid, the chambered nautilus, and cuttlefish. Cephalopods belong to another group of animals called mollusks.

chemoreceptors special nerve cells in an octopus's suckers that sense substances in the water

chromatophores special cells in the skin that let the octopus change its color

cirrata group name for octopuses that have rows of thin, hair-like organs on their arms instead of suckers

cryptic camouflage hiding by looking like the surroundings

den home of an octopus. A den can be a crack in a rock, a hole in the sand, or a space under a pile of rocks. A den can also be an empty seashell or an old can.

gills organs that fish and most other sea animals use for breathing

habitat place where an animal lives

ink dark liquid that an octopus sends out from an ink sac in its body when the octopus feels threatened

invertebrates animals that do not have back bones

mantle bag-like structure made of muscle that contains the heart, digestive system, and other internal organs of an octopus and other cephalopods

mantle cavity space between the inside of the mantle and the internal organs

midden pile of shells and other remains of animals an octopus has eaten and that it has left outside its den

mimicry looking and acting like something else. Mimicry is a form of camouflage.

mollusk kind of animal that does not have a back bone. Some mollusks, such as clams and snails, have shells to protect their soft bodies. Other mollusks, such as octopuses, do not have shells.

pelagic of the open ocean

plankton tiny plants and animals that float near the surface of the ocean

predator animal that hunts and eats other animals

prey animal that another animal hunts for food

radula the "tongue" of an octopus. The radula is covered with tiny, rough teeth.

ROV (Remotely Operated Vehicle) small robot submarine that scientists use for learning about the deep sea

school group of fish or other sea creatures that swim together

SCUBA (Self-Contained Underwater Breathing Apparatus) mouthpiece, hose, and air tanks. The tanks contain a mixture of gases so a diver can breathe underwater.

siphon tube inside the mantle that sends water out of the mantle cavity after the gills take oxygen from the water

species type of animal or plant

suckers round cups on the underside of an octopus arm that grab objects and also feel and taste the objects. Suckers are like suction cups.

webbing or web piece of skin that joins the arms of an octopus together under the mantle

More Books to Read

Markert, Jenny. *Octopuses*. Chanhassen, Minn.: Child's World, 2001.

Trueit, Trudi Strain. *Octopuses, Squids, and Cuttlefishes*. Danbury, Conn.: Franklin Watts, 2002.

Wu, Norbert and Leighton Taylor. *Octopuses*. New York: Lerner Publishing Group, 2002.

Index

Antarctic octopuses 12
arms 7, 8, 9, 11, 15, 21, 26, 28, 29

babies 22, 23–24
beak 7, 9, 14
benthic octopuses 12
blood 7, 8, 9
blue-ringed octopuses 19
body 6–9, 20, 28
brain 7, 29

Californian octopuses 10
camouflage 16
Caribbean reef octopuses 16
cephalopods 6
chemoreceptors 8
chromatophores 16
cirrate octopuses 11, 13
cirri 11
color 23, 29
common octopuses 10, 12, 29
cryptic camouflage 16

day octopuses 20
dens 13, 14, 20, 21, 22, 23
dwarf octopuses 22

eggs 22, 23, 26, 29
esophagus 28
eyes 7, 18

females 21, 22, 23, 26, 29
fins 11
food. See prey.

giant Pacific octopuses 4, 5, 6, 10, 12, 18, 23, 28
gills 7, 8

habitats 12–13, 16, 25
head 7
hearts 7, 8
hemocyanin 9

Incirrata octopuses 10
"ink," 5, 17, 23, 28–29
ink sac 17, 29
invertebrates 6, 27

jetting 20

life span 24

males 21, 28
mantle 7, 8, 15, 16, 17, 20, 21
mantle cavity 7, 20
marine biologists 4, 26
mating 21–23
middens 14, 15
mimicry 16
mollusks 6, 14
moray eels 15
mouth 8, 9

octopus hunting 15

pelagic octopuses 13
plankton 24
pollution 25
predators 15, 16, 17, 18, 19, 22
prey 14, 25

radula 14
red octopuses 21
research 5, 25, 26, 27
ROVs (Remotely Operated Vehicles) 26

saliva 14
schools 21
SCUBA (Self-Contained Underwater Breathing Apparatus) gear 4–5
siphon 7, 8, 20, 29
size 10
skin 16
species 10–11, 25, 27
suckers 7, 8, 9, 28, 29

tongue. See radula.

venom 19

webbing 9, 11